Harry Potter™

MAGIC EYE® BOOK
3D Magical Moments

3D Illusions by Magic Eye Inc.

Andrews McMeel
Publishing, LLC

Kansas City • Sydney • London

Harry Potter Magic Eye Book: 3D Magical Moments copyright © 2011 by Warner Bros. Entertainment Inc.
Magic Eye images copyright © 2011 by Magic Eye Inc. All rights reserved. Printed in China. No part of this book may be used
or reproduced in any manner whatsoever without written permission except in the case of reprints in the context of reviews.

Andrews McMeel Publishing, LLC
an Andrews McMeel Universal company
1130 Walnut Street, Kansas City, Missouri 64106

www.andrewsmcmeel.com

11 12 13 14 15 WKT 10 9 8 7 6 5 4 3 2 1

ISBN: 978-1-4494-0141-2
Magic Eye 3D Artists: Cheri Smith and Sam Jones
Project Coordinators: Cheri Smith, Magic Eye Inc., and Victoria Selover, Warner Bros. Consumer Products

—— ATTENTION: SCHOOLS AND BUSINESSES ——

Andrews McMeel books are available at quantity discounts with bulk purchase for educational, business, or sales
promotional use. For information, please e-mail the Andrews McMeel Publishing Special Sales Department:
specialsales@amuniversal.com

Magic Eye images are available for educational, business, or sales promotional use. For information, contact:
Magic Eye Inc., P.O. Box 1986, Provincetown, Massachusetts 02657
www.magiceye.com

INTRODUCTION

The Harry Potter series has captured the world's imagination with its boy hero, wizardry, and loyal friendships, all woven into a tale of good versus evil.

A Magic Eye picture is a 3D stereogram that gives viewers the illusion of life. By playing on the human eye's natural depth perception, Magic Eye images leap off of the page and provide an exciting way for people to see fabulous images become something more through the magic of 3D.

Magic Eye and Harry Potter came together in *3D Magical Creatures, Beasts and Beings*, and now they appear together again in *3D Magical Moments*. In this book, images from the Harry Potter movies rise magically from the page through a special, patented 3D technology.

Through a 3D image, readers can view Harry, Ron, and Hermione exploring the village of Hogsmeade, learning new spells at Hogwarts, encountering the Whomping Willow, and more.

The spellbinding and timeless 3D magical moments illustrated in this book will entertain Muggles, witches, and wizards alike.

3D VIEWING TECHNIQUES

INSTRUCTIONS #2
FOR DIVERGING YOUR EYES
(focusing beyond the image)
To reveal the hidden 3D illusion, hold the center of the image *right up to your nose*. It should be blurry. Focus as though you are looking *through* the image into the distance. *Very slowly* move the image away from your face until you begin to perceive depth. Now hold the page still and the hidden image will slowly appear.

MAGIC EYE "FLOATERS"
Magic Eye "Floaters" are another type of Magic Eye 3D illusion. "Floaters" can first be viewed in 2D, and then, by using the standard Magic Eye viewing techniques, "Floaters" will appear to float in 3D space. Floaters and Magic Eye hidden illusions may be combined. (See page 7.)

ADDITIONAL VIEWING INFORMATION
Discipline is needed when a Magic Eye 3D illusion starts to "come in" because at that moment you will instinctively try to look at the page rather than looking through it, or before it. If you "lose it," start again.

There are two methods for viewing Magic Eye images: diverging your eyes (focusing beyond the image) and converging your eyes (focusing before the image or crossing your eyes). All the Magic Eye images in this book have been created to be viewed by diverging your eyes.

INSTRUCTIONS #1
FOR DIVERGING YOUR EYES
(focusing beyond the image)
To reveal the hidden 3D illusion, hold the center of the image *right up to your nose*. It should be blurry. Focus as though you are looking *through*

the image into the distance. *Very slowly* move the image away from your face until the two squares above the image turn into three squares. If you see four squares, move the image farther away from your face until you see three squares. If you see one or two squares, start over!

When you *clearly see three squares*, hold the page still, and the hidden image will slowly appear. Once you perceive the hidden image and depth, you can look around the entire 3D image. The longer you look, the clearer it becomes. The farther away you hold the page, the deeper it becomes.

If you converge your eyes (focus before the image or cross your eyes) and view an image created for diverging your eyes, the depth information comes out backward, and vice versa! This means if we intend to show a dragon flying in front of a cloud, if you converge your eyes you will see a dragon-shaped hole cut into the cloud! Another common occurrence is to diverge or converge your eyes twice as far as is needed to see the hidden image; for example, when you see four squares above the image instead of three, you will see a scrambled version of the intended hidden image.

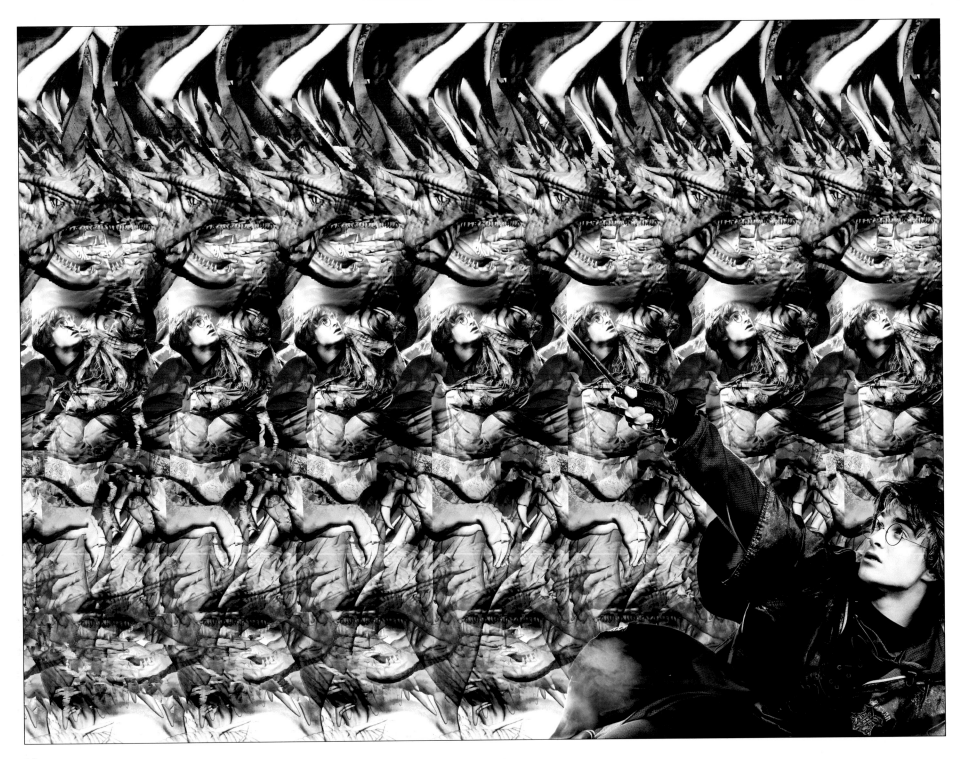

16

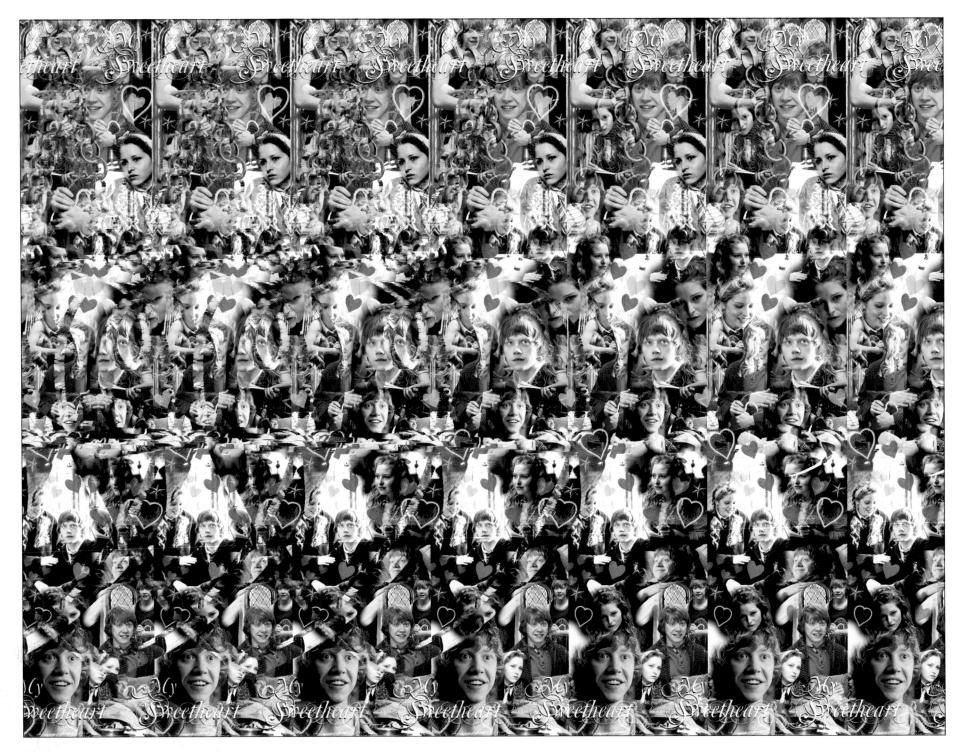

29

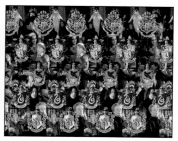
Book Cover
Hogwarts Crests

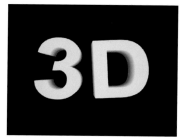
Page 4
3D Viewing Instructions

Page 5   Dumbledore's Army

Page 6   Aunt Marge
Floats Away

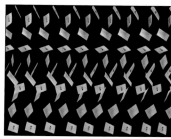
Page 7   Hogwarts Acceptance
Letter

Page 8   Hogwarts castle

Page 9   Wizard Chess

Page 10   Chocolate Frog

Page 11   Sorting Hat

Page 12   Weasleys' Flying Car

Page 13   Polyjuice Potion

Page 14   Quidditch (Harry on
his broom)

Page 15   Whomping Willow

Page 16   Hungarian Horntail

Page 17   Triwizard Cup

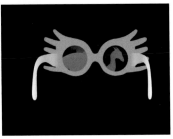

Page 18   Spectrespecs

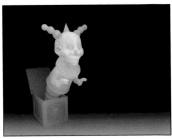

Page 19   Defense Against the
Dark Arts class (Boggart)

Page 20   The Yule Ball

Page 21   Hogsmeade

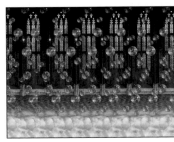

Page 22   Prefects' Bathroom
(3D Bubbles, 2D Harry with
the golden egg)

Page 23   Felix Felicis

Page 24   Lavender's Gift to
Ron (Heart Necklace)

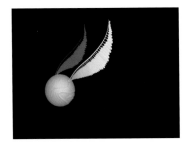

Page 25   Golden Snitch

Page 26   Sirius Black

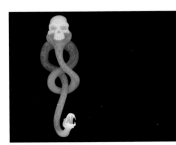

Page 27   Draco Becomes a
Death Eater

Page 28   Prophecy Orbs

Page 29   Dumbledore Battles
Voldermort

Page 30   Fireworks Dragon